The Feelings Friends

Written by Lindsey Perper
Illustrated by Sara Rutkowski

To Ella and Joey~

You both are my heart and soul.
Thank you for inspiring me every day. I am
so incredibly grateful for our little team.

For my Ella:
LYU Lulu

For my Joey:
I love you Google

It is a beautiful day on Feeling Street. Happy Harper, Sad Sam, and Mad Matthew are all playing basketball on the driveway.

Happy Harper feels so happy because she is spending time with her favorite friends. Sad Sam feels sad because he is missing his sister while she is away at camp. Mad Matthew feels mad because his mom wants him to come home soon and clean his messy room, but he wants to stay and play.

Happy Harper, Sad Sam, and Mad Matthew decide to go for a walk to the park (they ask their parents first, of course!). Along the way, they are hoping to see some friends.

Excited Ella and Joyful Joey are the first friends they bump into on their walk. As brother and sister, Excited Ella and Joyful Joey have a lot in common. They are feeling excited and joyful because they are doing so many things they love on this beautiful day!

6

As the friends continue on their walk together, they all see Embarrassed Emily hiding behind a bush. Embarrassed Emily doesn't want her friends to see her because she got a haircut today, and she doesn't like the way her curls stick up all over the place now. She is hoping her friends don't see her.

Confident Carson comes skipping across the street (after looking both ways first, of course). He tells Embarrassed Emily, "It doesn't matter to me what anyone else says. I think you look awesome. Look at MY hair - it's silly too. But it doesn't matter to me what anyone thinks because I feel good about myself JUST the way I am!"

Frustrated Frank comes walking out of his house just then and trips on his shoelace. Just after he ties it and starts walking again, his laces come untied and he trips - again! Frustrated Frank is feeling very frustrated because he can't get his shoelace to stay tied. He finally double knots his laces, and then he doesn't feel so frustrated anymore.

Lonely Lexi is sitting on her front porch watching all of the friends laughing and having fun. She is feeling very alone. Her big dog Tiny comes to join her, but she still wishes that her friends would come over and ask her to play with them.

Scared Scarlett sees her friends and decides to join them on their walk. But as soon as they round the corner near Lonely Lexi's house, Scared Scarlett spots the big dog. She feels scared of the big dog that she has never met before. Lonely Lexi asks if Scared Scarlett wants to come pet Tiny the big dog.

Brave Becca isn't afraid of Tiny the big dog. Brave Becca holds Scared Scarlett's hand, and they gently pet the big dog together. Tiny is very friendly, so Scared Scarlett doesn't feel so scared anymore.

Finally, all of the friends arrive at the park. They are all so happy to see Proud Penelope - she has been working so very hard for many weeks to get across the monkey bars. And today - for the first time - Proud Penelope makes it ALL the way across! She feels so very proud of herself for never giving up.

Unfortunately, Jealous Jack hasn't practiced hard enough, and he keeps falling off of the monkey bars. It is okay that Jealous Jack can't do the monkey bars yet - all of his friends know that he will learn soon. He wants to be happy for Proud Penelope, but all Jealous Jack feels is jealousy. He feels like he can't be happy for her because he wants to be able to do what she can do.

As the sun sets on Feeling Street, all of the friends head home to their families. They all feel cheerful because they have had such a fun day spending time together!

24

Happy, sad, mad, excited, joyful, confident, frustrated, lonely, scared, brave, proud, jealous, and cheerful are just a few of the feelings we feel. We all feel many different ways on many different days. Whoever you are and whatever you feel is A-OK as long as you know what you're feeling.

How do YOU feel today?

About the Author:

Lindsey is a mom, a Licensed Clinical Social Worker, a Certified Life Coach, and a Nationally Certified Parenting Coordinator. She has been in private practice as a behavioral therapist for over 13 years. Lindsey owns her practice and enjoys the balance of work and home.

She has two incredibly amazing kids- Ella and Joey. Lindsey loves yoga, sushi, reading, watching Ella dance on stage, and watching Joey on the soccer field and basketball court! Someone very special encouraged Lindsey to combine her passion for her work, for expressing emotions, and for children; and so, this book was born!

Please enjoy~

About the Illustrator:

Sara is a Chicago-based illustrator who loves drawing cartoons for both children and adults. She received her Bachelor of Fine Arts in Illustration from the American Academy of Art in 2015. When Sara isn't cartooning, she delves in graphic design, watercolor painting, and colored pencil drawings.

Visit her website www.sararutkowski.com
to see more of her work!

Made in the USA
Charleston, SC
26 May 2016